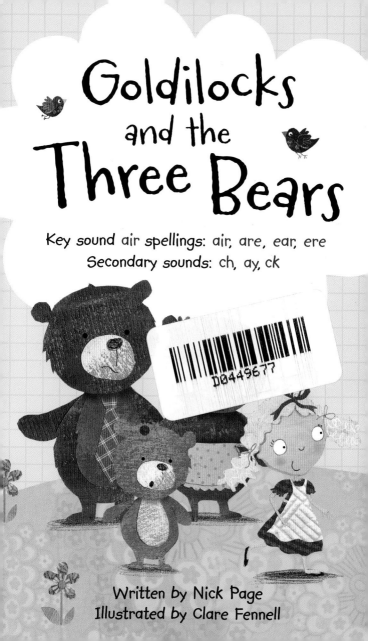

Goldilocks
and the
Three Bears

Key sound air spellings: air, are, ear, ere
Secondary sounds: ch, ay, ck

D0449677

Written by Nick Page
Illustrated by Clare Fennell

Reading with phonics

How to use this book

The **Reading with phonics** series helps you to have fun with your child and to support their learning of phonics and reading. It is aimed at children who have learned the letter sounds and are building confidence in their reading.

Each title in the series focuses on a different key sound. The entertaining retelling of the story repeats this sound frequently, and the different spellings for the sound are highlighted in red type. The first activity at the back of the book provides practice in reading and using words that contain this sound. The key sound for **Goldilocks and the Three Bears** is **air**.

Start by reading the story to your child, asking them to join in with the refrain in bold. Next, encourage them to read the story with you. Give them a hand to decode tricky words.

Now look at the activity pages at the back of the book. These are intended for you and your child to enjoy together. Most are not activities to complete in pencil or pen, but by reading and talking or pointing.

The **Key sound** pages focus on one sound, and on the various different groups of letters that produce that sound. Encourage your child to read the different letter groups and complete the activity, so they become more aware of the variety of spellings there are for the same sound.

The **Letters together** pages look at three pairs or groups of letters and at the sounds they make as they work together. Help your child to read the words and trace the route on the word maps.

Rhyme is used a lot in these retellings. Whatever stage your child has reached in their learning of phonics, it is always good practice for them to listen carefully for sounds and find words that rhyme. The pages on **Rhyming words** take six words from the story and ask children to read and find other words that rhyme with them.

The **Sight words** pages focus on a number of sight words that occur regularly but can nonetheless be challenging. Many of these words are not sounded out following the rules of phonics and the easiest thing is for children to learn them by sight, so that they do not worry about decoding them. These pages encourage children to retell the story, practicing sight words as they do so.

The **Picture dictionary** page asks children to focus closely on nine words from the story. Encourage children to look carefully at each word, cover it with their hand, write it on a separate piece of paper, and finally, check it!

Do not complete all the activities at once – doing one each time you read will ensure that your child continues to enjoy the stories and the time you are spending together. **Have fun!**

In a house in the woods (who knows where?),
live Ma and Pa and Mary Bear.
While their porridge cools in the morning air,
they fetch some cream from the dairy.

Oh, bears, beware! Oh, bears, beware!
Beware of girls with golden hair!

Goldilocks with long, fair hair
finds the house – there's no one there –
and walks straight in – she doesn't care!
She doesn't find it scary.

Oh, bears, beware! Oh, bears, beware!
Beware of girls with golden hair!

She sees the porridge, all prepared.
"Too hot! Too cold!" the girl declares.
But one's just right, and then and there,
she takes the one for Mary.

Oh, *bears*, beware! Oh, *bears*, beware!
Beware of girls with golden hair!

And then she tries out all the chairs.

"Too hard! Too soft!" the girl despairs.

She squeezes into Mary's chair
and breaks it! How contrary!

Oh!

Oh, bears, beware! Oh, bears, beware!
Beware of girls with golden hair!

And now she makes her way upstairs
to try the beds of those three bears.

"Too high! Too low!" But over there –
the bed of little Mary.

Oh, bears, beware!
Oh, bears, beware!
Beware of girls
with golden hair!

Zzzz!

The bears return – they're soon aware
that someone's tried their breakfast fare.
"My porridge is gone," says Mary Bear.
"Perhaps it was a fairy!"

Oh, bears, beware! Oh, bears, beware!
Beware of girls with golden hair!

And then they see the broken chair,
with bits of wood spread everywhere.
It's ruined, quite beyond repair.

"I loved that chair,"
says Mary.

Oh, bears, beware! Oh, bears, beware!
Beware of girls with golden hair!

17

They hear a sound, and creep upstairs.

"Who's there?" says Pa.

"Come out, who dares!"

In Mary's bed – oh, how they stare:

a girl, all golden-hairy!

ZZZZZzz!

Oh, bears, beware! Oh, bears, beware!

Beware of girls with golden hair!

"You porridge thief!" shouts Mommy Bear,
which gives the girl a dreadful scare!
She runs so fast away from there,
from Ma and Pa and Mary!

Oh, bears, beware! Oh, bears, beware!
Beware of girls with golden hair!

A word to small girls everywhere:
don't try the bed or break the chair,
and never, ever, dare to share
the porridge of little Mary!

Oh, bears, beware! Oh, bears, beware!
Beware of girls with golden hair!

Key sound

There are several different groups of letters that make the **air** sound. Practice them by helping Mary Bear make some sentences. Use each word in the balloons in a different sentence.

fair
chair
hair
pair

share
care
bare
scare
hare
stare

pear
wear
bear
tear

there
where

Now can you make a
sentence with one word
from each of the balloons?

Letters together

Look at these pairs of letters and say the sounds they make.

ch   ay   ck

Follow the words that contain **ch** to help Mary Bear find her chair.

ch

waves

chips   child

chick

from   lost

cheerful

jumps   chair   right

Follow the words that contain **ay** to help the bears chase Goldilocks away!

ay

the

tray

day

play

stay

way

other

say

away

lots

Follow the words that contain **ck** to find a naughty girl called Goldilocks!

ck

rock

sock

suddenly

block

knock

beautiful

other

Goldilocks

Rhyming words

Read the words in the flowers and point to other words that rhyme with them.

three	**walk**	chalk
talk		soft

low	**know**	chair
throw		eats

tear	**bear**	wear
roof		table

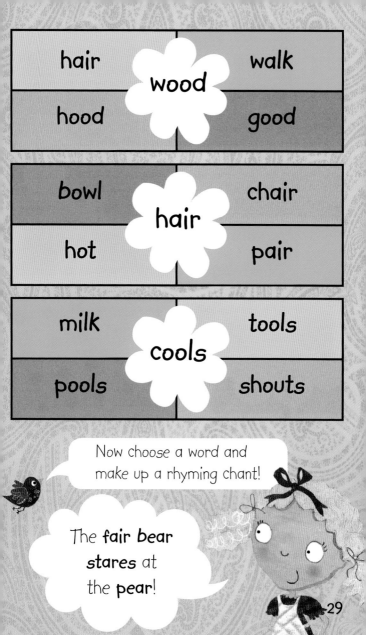

hair

wood

walk

hood

good

bowl

hair

chair

hot

pair

milk

cools

tools

pools

shouts

Now choose a word and make up a rhyming chant!

The **fair bear stares** at the **pear**!

29

Sight words

Many common words can be difficult to sound out. Practice them by reading these sentences about the story. Now make more sentences using other sight words from around the border.

The bears chased Goldilocks **out.**

Goldilocks went into the bears' **house.**

Goldilocks **sat** in all of the chairs.

The bears **came** home and saw Goldilocks.

have • my

• very • day • don't • he • all • morning • came • each

A girl **called** Goldilocks came along.

The bears made breakfast in the **morning**.

Mary was a **little** bear.

Goldilocks tried **each** bowl of porridge.

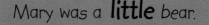

Goldilocks went to **sleep**.

before • little • am • tell • key • place • sat • sleep • when • called • which • run • any

its • that • like • out • what • called • looked • house •

Picture dictionary

Look carefully at the pictures and the words.
Now cover the words, one at a time.
Can you remember how to write them?

bear

bed

broken

chair

girl

hair

house

porridge

woods